Tomatoes
and Other Killer Vegetable Jokes and Riddles

by
Stephanie Johnson
Illustrated by Jack White

TOR

A TOM DOHERTY ASSOCIATES BOOK
NEW YORK

This is a work of fiction. All the characters and events portrayed in this book are fictitious, and any resemblance to real people or events is purely coincidental.

TOMATOES AND OTHER KILLER VEGETABLE JOKES AND RIDDLES

Copyright © 1992 by RGA Publishing Group, Inc.

A Tor Book
Published by Tom Doherty Associates, Inc.
49 West 24th Street
New York, N.Y. 10010

TOR ® is a registered trademark of Tom Doherty Associates, Inc.

Cover and interior art by Jack White

ISBN:0-812-51995-7

First edition: February 1992

Printed in the United States of America

0 9 8 7 6 5 4 3 2 1

What happens when a rotten tomato attends a fruit and vegetable meeting?
　He raises a stink.

Why are tomatoes named tomatoes?
　Because that's what everybody calls them.

Why are so many tomatoes out of work?
　Because they're always getting canned.

How do you make a big squash?
Drop a tomato off the Empire State Building.

How many tomatoes can you put in an empty sack?
One. After that the sack isn't empty.

What did the boy tomato say to the girl tomato?
Nothing. Tomatoes can't talk.

What do you call a pet tomato?
You can call it anything you want, but it won't hear you.

Where do tomatoes sleep at night?
In the garden bed, and under sheets of rain and blankets of fog.

Why did the tomato hide from the knife?
He didn't want to get the point.

Husband: Where are you going?
Wife: Out to water the tomatoes.
Husband: But it's raining outside!
Wife: Don't worry, I'll wear my raincoat.

How do you fix a broken tomato?
  With tomato paste.

A mother tomato and three baby tomatoes
were walking down the street one afternoon.
The mother tomato looked back over her
shoulder and saw that the littlest tomato was
way behind the others. The mother yelled,
"Hurry up, little tomato," and kept walking.
Soon the mother tomato looked over her
shoulder again. The littlest tomato was even
farther behind this time. The mother tomato
yelled, "Hurry up, little tomato," and kept
walking. Later, the mother tomato looked over
her shoulder once more and saw that the littlest
tomato was way, WAY behind. The mother
tomato went over to the littlest tomato and
stomped all over him, saying, "CATCH-UP!!"

Where can you find baby corns?
  In corn cribs.

What's green and lives in salt water?
  Moby Pickle.

What do corn cobs carry in their wallets?
  Corn "bread."

How do you divide ten tomatoes evenly among nine people?

Make tomato sauce.

Boy: I wish I had enough money to buy a million tomatoes.
Girl: What would you do with a million tomatoes?
Boy: Nothing. I just want the money.

If I had six tomatoes in one hand and seven in the other, what would I have?

Large hands.

Why wouldn't the woman buy tomatoes at 5 cents a piece?

She wanted whole ones.

Why is it possible to preserve tomatoes longer these days?

Because we can.

There are two piles of tomatoes in the left corner, and three piles in the right corner. If the grocer puts them all together, what will he have?
One big pile.

Why did the corn call the tomato lazy?
Because it was always hanging out in its bed.

What's red and goes up and down?
A tomato in an elevator.

Why don't tomatoes laugh?
With all of these terrible tomato jokes going around, how could they?

What happens when a green tomato is put into very cold water?
It gets wet.

Why are tomatoes like books?
They're red. (read)

What do you call a bean that joins the armed forces?
A Navy bean.

What's purple and conquered the world?
Alexander the Grape.

What kind of TV shows do bananas often star in?
Breakfast serials.

What's yellow, ugly, and scares villagers?
  Frankensquash.

What is the best thing to put into an apple pie?
  Your teeth!

Why do potatoes make good detectives?
  They always have their eyes peeled.

What's green, wrinkled, and famous for its beauty?
  The Mona Lettuce. (Mona Lisa)

What's green and goes through walls?
  Casper the Friendly Cucumber.

Where do baby corns come from?
  The stalk brings them.

What's long and yellow and wears diapers?
  A baby banana.

What's thin and green and dances well?
  Fred Asparagus.

What did the baby corn ask the mama corn?
  "Where's pop corn?"

Why should you keep comedians away from
egg farms?
  Because the eggs will crack up.

What do all gardeners grow?
  Old.

Why did the pickle see a psychologist?
  He went through a jarring experience.

What vegetables can sometimes be found in
people's shoes?
  Corns.

How many bananas should you get for a dollar?
  None. Dollars don't eat bananas.

What kind of vegetables do chickens like best?
  Eggplants.

What fruit will give you a jolt?
  Currant.

Chicken house motto: An egg a day keeps the axe away.

What do you call a head of lettuce, two tomatoes, and a cucumber jumping on a trampoline?
  A tossed salad.

Why is a corn field like an army?
  It's full of kernels.

Why should you treat every apple like royalty?
  One might be a Duchess.

What kind of vegetable is like old paint?
  A potato. It peels and chips.

Why did the farmer sell his chickens?
He didn't need them because he already had plenty of eggplants.

What's the difference between an elephant and spaghetti?
An elephant doesn't slip off the end of your fork.

What's orange and wears a mask?
The Lone Tangerine.

What did the pickle say to the dealer?
"Dill me in."

Where does a monkey sleep?
In an ape-ri-cot.

What do you get when you upholster a potato?
A couch potato.

What does a cold cow give?
  Ice cream.

What can you put into a bag of potatoes to make it weigh less?
  A hole.

Knock, knock,
Who's there?
Lettuce.
Lettuce who?
Lettuce in, it's cold outside.

Why do bananas use sunblock?
  Because they peel.

What do leopards say when they finish lunch?
  "That hit the spots."

How do you make a fruit stand?
  Take away its chair.

What did the celery stick say to the broccoli spear?
  "Shall we go for a dip?"

Why can't you eat carrots with fingers?
  Carrots don't have fingers.

What happened when the corn kernels got into a fight?
   They all got creamed.

What's green and sour and always changing its mind?
   A fickle pickle.

Where do wealthy apples keep their money?
   In a branch bank.

Why was the artichoke mad?
   The cook had him steamed.

Why did the lettuce slap the stale bread?
   The bread was trying to get fresh.

What did the girl say to the corn cob?
   "It was nice gnawing (knowing) you."

Where do peanuts hang out?
   At the candy bar.

What's orange and buzzes?
An electric carrot.

What did the prune say when it defeated the grape?
"I Concord (conquered) grape."

Why do elephants eat peanuts?
Because watermelons get stuck in their trunks.

What did the onion say when it was boiled in the stew?
"I'm not as strong as I used to be."

Customer: Waiter, this lobster has only one claw.
Waiter: Yes, sir, that proves how fresh our lobsters are. They fight with each other in the kitchen.
Customer: Well, go back into the kitchen and bring me the winner.

What did the mother werewolf say to her son?
  "Quit wolfing down your food."

What do you call a potato that works as a sports announcer?
  A common-tater (commentator)

Why did the corn salute the refrigerator?
The corn was a kernel but the refrigerator was a General Electric.

How do you make a lemon drop?
Let it fall.

Why did the tree steal the apple's clothes?
It wanted to bare fruit.

Why did the raspberry call his attorney?
He was in a jam.

Why did the farmer install a jacuzzi in his chicken house?
His wife wanted her hard-boiled eggs to be as fresh as possible.

What do you call a cucumber with a sour disposition?
A pickle.

Why did the egg say, "Oh, neat"?
It was just an eggs-pression.

What kind of nut can you hang a picture on?
A walnut

Which end of a carrot is the left end?
The end you don't eat.

What is the last vegetable in the alphabet?
Zucchini.

How do chicks fit inside their eggs?
Eggs-actly.

What was purple and ruled the waves?
Grape Britain.

What fruit is the most up-to-date?
Currant.

What do you call the rear door of a cafeteria?
The back-teria.

What carries its heart in its head?
Lettuce.

What's purple and stamps out forest fires?
Smokey the Grape.

What is the most expensive cookie?
A fortune cookie.

Larry: Did I tell you the joke about the banana
    peel?
Mary: It seems to have slipped my mind.

*What's orange, hangs from a tree, and has
fangs?*
A saber-toothed kumquat.

What do you call a pear that plays the trumpet?
  A tootie-fruitie.

What's lemonade?
  When you help an old lemon across the street.

What's white, fluffy, and beats its chest in a pastry shop?
   A meringue-utan.

Why did the egg crack?
   He got a little over-egg-cited.

How can you tell if a gardener is rich?
   He has a 24-carrot (karat) garden.

What kind of jokes do corn cobs tell?
   Corny ones.

What kind of beans do horses like best?
   Pinto beans.

Girl: Why did the man call his wife a peach?
Boy: Because she was sweet?
Girl: No, because she had a heart of stone.

What do apple actors play?
   "Bit" parts.

What kind of toes do you find in the ground?
  Pota-toes.

Why did the math teacher dice her carrots?
  She wanted square roots.

Why was the bread spread asked to leave the concession line?
  He was a "butter."

What's the pickle capital of the United States?
  Dill-adelphia.

If two men, two women, two boys, and two girls went to a restaurant, how many dined?
  Eight ate.

What's the best way to raise turnips?
  Take hold of the tops and pull!

What part of a fish weighs the most?
  The scales.

Why did the lemon run and hide?
Because he was yellow-bellied.

What do you call a monster café?
A beastro.

What kind of vegetable has borrowed everything it has?
A lentil. (lent-all)

Why do gardeners keep getting richer?
Because their celery (salary) keeps growing.

Student: Is it better to do homework on a full or an empty stomach?
Teacher: Neither. It's best to do homework on paper.

Why did the astronaut sit down to eat?
It was launch time.

Why did the orange juice flunk out of school?
  It wouldn't concentrate.

Which apple will a man buy?
  Whichever he "chews."

What do bowlers eat?
  Spare ribs.

Why did the mother lollipop spank her son?
  He was due for a licking.

What did the nearsighted gingerbread man need for his eyes?
  Contact raisins.

What's green and blue and goes to the doctor?
  A cucumber with frostbite.

Why is a supermarket owner worse than a slob?
  A slob is gross, but a supermarket owner is grocer.

What salad is best for honeymooners?
    Lettuce alone.

*How do you serve tomato soup to a football
player?*
    In a souper-bowl.

When is an Irish potato not Irish?
  When it's French fried.

Why shouldn't you tell a secret in a cornfield?
  Because there are too many ears.

What does an orange do when it gets a cold?
  It squeezes.

What kind of fruit does Count Dracula like best?
  Neck-tarines.

If a butcher were 6 feet tall and wore a size 10 apron, what would he weigh?
  Meat.

What's rhubarb?
  Celery with high blood pressure.

What happened to the dog that ate garlic?
  Its bark was worse than its bite.

Dairy man: Why are you so tired?

Farmer: Well, there isn't that much money in milk these days, so I sat up all night trying to think of something else for my cows to do.

What cake makes its own eggs?
  A layer cake.

How do you speak to a hot dog?
  Frankly.

What do sprinters eat?
  Fast food.

How many peas are there in a pint?
  There is only one "P."

What happens when peas are arrested?
  They come along peas-fully.

What did the little chick say when it found an orange in its nest?
 "Look at the orange Mama laid!" (marmalade)

What do you call a shrimp market?
 A prawn shop.

Girl: Did you hear about the baby that ate nothing but corn for two weeks and gained ten pounds?
Boy: No, whose baby was it?
Girl: A cow's!

Why did the corncob go to the doctor?
 She had an earache.

What do you get when you cross a cucumber with a lemon?
 A sour pickle.

Where were French fries first made?
 In Greece. (grease)

Why didn't the orange finish the race?
It ran out of juice.

What happens when a rotten tomato attends a fruit and vegetable meeting?
He raises a stink.

Can a pea box?
No, but a tomato can.

Why do tomatoes turn red?
You'd turn red too if you had to change outdoors!

How do you keep a rotten tomato from smelling?
Hold its nose.

How do you make a tomato stew?
Keep it waiting for a long, long time.

Where can you find tomatoes no matter what time of year it is?
In the dictionary.

What do you call a perfect egg?
  Eggs-act.

Why is bread like the sun?
  It rises from the yeast.

What do you call an adventuresome egg?
  An eggs-plorer.

What vegetable hurts if you step on it?
    Corn.

What kind of nut uses suntan lotion?
    A beech nut.

What does a snowman eat for lunch?
    Cold cuts.

Why was the cookie homesick?
    Because he was a "wafer" so long.

If William Penn's aunts owned a pie shop, what would they call their prices?
    The pie-rates of Penn's aunts.

What is a witch's favorite cereal?
    Scream of Wheat.

What do you call an egg that goes too far?
    An eggs-tremist.

What do you get when a pea picks a fight with a potato?
   A black-eyed pea.

What vegetable do squirrels like best?
   Acorn squash.

What's stranger than seeing a turkey roll?
   Watching a clam bake.

What do you call an ignorant bean?
   A green bean.

What do you call a baby hot dog?
   A teenie weenie.

What do you call a stolen candy bar?
   Hot chocolate.

Did Adam and Eve ever have a date?
No, but they had an apple.

What is a buccaneer?
Too much to pay for corn.

Why are bananas never lonely?
They hang out in bunches.

What is a shark's favorite ice cream?
Toothy fruity.

What do basketball players eat?
  Chicken in the basket.

Teacher: If I had ten oranges and gave you five,
    how many would I have left?
Student: I don't know, I learned with apples.

Why do figs like February?
  Because there are less dates to compete with.

What does a banana do when it sees a monkey approaching?
  It splits!

Where can you find a man eating fish?
  In a seafood restaurant.

Customer: Do you have any vegetarian dishes on the menu?
Waiter: We did, but I wiped them off.

How can you get rich in the candy business?
By making a mint.

What do you call a cucumber that toots?
A pickle-o.

How do we know that carrots are good for our eyes?
Because rabbits don't wear eyeglasses.

Why did the sailor sail his boat into the orange grove?
He was looking for the "Vitamin Sea."

How do you silence a ham?
Take away his microphone.

What branch of the military do worms serve in?
The Apple Corps.

What do cheerleaders eat?
  Cheer-ios.

What do you call a dinosaur egg?
  Egg-stinct.

If a boat had 19 holes in it, why didn't it sink?
  The holes were in the sailors' Swiss cheese.

What happened to the tomato that the monster planted?
  It grue-some.

What did the tomato say to the rotten lettuce?
  "You should have your head examined."

What did the hen say when she saw a plate of scrambled eggs?
  "What crazy mixed-up kids!"

What did the egg say to the cook?
  "One more crack like that and the yolk's on you!"

What can you do for a blueberry?
  Try to cheer it up.

Professor: I once had to live on a jar of peanut
    butter for a whole week!
Student: Really? Where do you live now?

*What kind of beans do anatomy teachers like
best?*
  Kidney beans.

*What do you call a yam with a wonderful
personality?*
  A sweet potato.

Customer: Waiter, I don't see any peas in my
    pea soup.
Waiter: Well, that's because they all split.

What do you call a very angry muffin?
  A hot cross bun.

Why did the mother peanut bring her son to a psychiatrist?

He wouldn't come out of his shell.

What do eggs do when they see the frying pan approaching?

Scramble.

What do you call a hamburger dance?
A meat ball.

What did the doughnut say to the pound cake?
"If I had your dough, I wouldn't hang around this hole."

How do you get milk from Moscow?
Go into the barn next to Pa's cow.

When do you give a vegetable the Heimlich maneuver?
When Artie-chokes. (artichokes)

What room has no walls, no ceiling, and no floor?
A mushroom.

What did the egg say to the mixer?
"I'm beat."

Do you know what a balanced diet is?
  Sure, one apple in each hand.

Where were the first Idaho potatoes grown?
  In the ground.

Customer: I'd like a double chocolate sundae
    with lots of whipped cream.
Waiter: Would you like a cherry on that?
Customer: Heavens, no, I'm on a diet.

What do you get when you put three ducks in a crate?
  A box of quackers.

How do horses stay so thin?
  Because they only eat when there isn't a bit
  in their mouths.

What do you call a very large eggplant?
A chicken farm.

What do you feed a duck for breakfast?
Quacker oats.

What's green and sour and gives presents at Christmas?
Santa Pickle.

What do you call two hamburgers dueling it out in the alley behind a café?
A meat brawl.

Did you hear about the woman who couldn't stop talking?
She had alphabet soup for lunch and the words just kept coming out of her mouth.

Where do dates grow?
  On calendar trees.

Why did the farmer feed the cow money?
  To get rich milk.

Woman: Grocer, I sent my daughter for 10 pounds of pickles, but she only came home with 5. Is your scale correct?

Grocer: Yes, ma'am, my scale is correct. Have you weighed your daughter?

Where do turkeys go before their Thanksgiving dance appearance?

To the dressing room.

What did the cook say when the pancake came out bumpy?

"That's waffle." (awful)

Why are peanuts brown?

So you can tell them apart from watermelons.

What did the bakery owner say to the bread baker?

"Quit loafing."

What do you call a crowded mushroom?
  Stuffed.

Are peanuts fattening?
  Have you ever seen a skinny elephant?

What's worse than a blind date?
  A deaf prune.

What happens when you step on a grape?
  It lets out a little whine. (wine)

What makes pies sneaky?
  The letter S will make spies of them.

Why is Miss Muffet's spider such a nuisance?
  Because it keeps getting in the whey.

Why are moths always hungry?
  They only eat holes.

What's red and goes slam, slam, slam, slam?
A four-door tomato.

What's red, then purple, then red, then purple?
A tomato that works part-time as a grape.

What's red and goes putt, putt?
An outboard tomato.

Mother: Did you eat the grapes?
Child: I didn't touch one of them!
Mother: Then why is there only one left?
Child: That's the one I didn't touch.

What has one mouth, two eyes, and three ears?
Someone eating corn on the cob.

What's the best way to keep mushrooms?
Don't give them away.

What vegetable do drummers like best?
Beets.

Customer: Waiter, do you serve shrimps here?
Waiter: Yes, we serve everyone regardless of
their size.

How does a ghost eat a candied apple?
By gobblin' it.

What are the smartest vegetables?
  Harvard beets.

Why is it impossible to get a consensus at a fruit and vegetable meeting?
  Because the cabbage leaves and the banana splits.

Why is an onion like a ringing bell?
  It keeps peeling.

Why do cabbages make good racers?
  They're always a-head.

What stays hot even in the refrigerator?
  Peppers.

What do you call a grouchy apple?
  A crab apple.

What did one olive say to the other?
  "Isn't life the pits?"

*What did the boy bunny give the girl bunny on
their engagement day?*
 A whole carrot. (karat)

Little girl: I feel like a banana.
Little boy: Funny, you don't look like one.

What is a monster's favorite food?
 Ghoul-ash.

Patient: Do you think spinach leaves are
     healthy?
Doctor: I've never heard them complain about
     their health.

What's a dog's favorite snack?
  Pupcorn.

*How do you turn one pail of corn into five pails
of corn?*
  Pop it.

Teacher: If you had three apples, and your
     mother told you to share them with your
     brother, how many would you give him?
Student: Do you mean my big brother or my
     little brother?

What did the grapevine say to the farmer?
  "Quit picking on me."

How do you get the water into a watermelon?
  Plant it in the spring.

What do you call a dog that eats watermelons?
  Melon-collie. (melancholy)

What kind of shoes do bananas wear?
  Slippers.

Where do you find religious grapes?
  Divine. (the vine)

If you have three pickles and I ask you to give me one, how many will you have?
  Three.

What do you call baggage in the trunk of a taxi cab?
  Cabbage.

What vegetable is as big as a city block?
  A policeman's beat. (beet)

How is an old potato chip like a mouse going into its hole?
You can see it's stale. (tail)

What kind of beans do monsters like best?
Human beans.

What do you call a scuba-diving hen?
Chicken of the sea.

For whom does the bell pepper toll?
His sweet pepper.

Why are olives jealous of their pits?
Because the pits are always getting taken out.

Why was the pastry chef arrested?
She was whipping the cream and beating the eggs.

Why shouldn't you let a banana borrow your dad's sports car?
Because it'll peel out.

Why did the farmer invite his ducks to dine with him?
He likes quackers with his soup.

What do you call a cow with calluses?
Corned beef.

Why don't musicians like tuna fish sandwiches?
   Because you can tune a piano, but you can't
   tune-a-fish.

Little girl: Do you like spinach?
Little boy: Yes.
Little girl: Good, then you can have mine.

What vegetable should you never take out on a boat?
   A leek.

Why shouldn't you tell a bean a secret?
   Because beans-talk.

Father: Eat your broccoli. It will put color in
   your cheeks.
Boy: Who wants green cheeks?

What's green and plays the guitar?
   Elvis Parsley.

Why was the bread expelled from school?
    He was always trying to butter up the teacher.

Customer: Waiter, why is my food so tough?
Waiter: Because you ordered filet of sole.

Why do hard-boiled eggs make good fighters?
    A hard-boiled egg is hard to beat.

What do you call a doughnut with a dazed expression on its face?
Glazed.

Why did the gardener drive a steamroller through his garden?
He wanted to grow mashed potatoes.

Knock, knock.
Who's there?
Fu Man Chu.
Fu Man Chu who?
Fu Man Chu food the way you do.

How do dogs like their eggs?
Pooched.

Why did the girl eat the banana skin?
It was a-peeling.

What can you do with bleu cheese?
Try to cheer it up.

How do you put together a soda-pop choir?
  With a little Coke-sing.

What do prize-fighters eat?
  Boxed lunches.

What kind of vegetables can you find at the North Pole?
  Chilly (chili) beans and iceberg lettuce.

What is Lassie's favorite vegetable?
  Collie-flower. (cauliflower)

Why did the lettuce blush?
  It saw the salad dressing.

What do ninja warriors like to eat?
  Chops.

What do ninja warriors like to drink?
  Carrot tea. (karate)

How much ice cream can a pine tree use?
Enough to fill up all its cones.

Can a turnip put air in a tire?
No, but a pump-kin.

When is a squash not a vegetable?
When it's a verb.

Have you ever seen cheese smoke?
   No, but I've seen a cream puff.

Customer: Waiter, what is this fly doing in my
      alphabet soup?
Waiter: Learning to read.

What letter is a vegetable?
   P. (pea)

When is roast beef highest in price?
   When it is rarest.

*How do you know when you've had too much
to eat?*
   When the person sitting next to you is you!

*Where did the ice-cream man learn to scoop ice
cream?*
   At Sundae school.

Why does a baker live without necessities?
  He's always selling what he kneads.

Why is popcorn like a bloodhound?
  They both smell good.

What did the leftovers say?
  "Foiled again."

What did the grape say as he was squeezed into juice?
  "I've got a pressing engagement."

How do you stop a watermelon leak?
  Get a melon patch, quick!

What happens when a cabbage improves her life-style?
  She turns over a new leaf.

What did the cherry say as it slid down the giraffe's throat?
  "Soooo long!"

Why did the boy eat the dollar bill?
It was his lunch money.

What must an actress do when playing a gardener?
  Mind her peas and cues.

How do you tease an egg?
  Egg it on.

Which would make a better fighter, a radish or a cherry?
  A cherry. Have you ever seen a fruit punch?

How far can you walk into a cornfield?
  Halfway. After that you're on your way out.

What looks like half an apple?
  The other half.

What should you do if you're attacked by an army of peanuts?
  Shell them.

Sausage link: Did you hear about the two
    sausages that met on the rotisserie?
Sausage patty: No, what happened?
Sausage link: They've been going around ever
    since.

Why did the apple cider call the police?
  It got "mugged."

What kind of sandwich can't be trusted?
  One that's full of baloney.

Why shouldn't you put vinegar in your ear?
  You could get pickled "hearing." (herring)

Why are berries often late for work?
  They're always getting into jams.

Which cabbage is the most conceited?
  The one with the biggest head.

Who was the most famous pickle gangster?
  Dill-inger.

What did the mother pig say to her son?
  "Quit making a hog of yourself!"

Baker: Do you like raisin bread?
Farmer: Can't say I ever tried raisin' bread.

Little girl: What's the best way to lick an ice cream cone?

Little boy: I don't know, I never fought an ice cream cone.

Knock, knock.
Who's there?
Mayonnaise.
Mayonnaise who?
"Mayonnaise have seen the glory . . ."

What do ghosts eat for dinner?
Spook-ghetti.

What do ghosts like for dessert?
Boo-berry pie.

What do ghosts eat with their boo-berry pie?
I-scream.

What do ghosts eat if they can't get boo-berry pie?
Angel food cake.

What has one horn and gives milk?
  A milk truck.

What do you get from a crazy hen?
  Scrambled eggs.

Did you hear the joke about the corn meal?
  Never mind, it's a lot of mush.

What do you call a potato that gets sunburned once and doesn't learn?
  Twice-baked.

How do gymnasts season their food?
  With somer-salt.

Why are bulls richer than cows?
  Cows give you milk, bulls charge you.

What food do body builders like best?
  Mussels.

Why did the detective interrogate the egg?
  To get it to crack.

Why did the gardener call a plumber?
  Because he saw a leek.

What did Eve say to Adam when it was time to go?
  "Lettuce (let us) leave."

What did the carrot say to the celery?
  "Quit stalking me!"

What do you call a squash with no courage?
  Yellow.

Why did the soda pop give in?
  He was a "soft" drink.

What happens when you pick a fight with a cow?
  You get creamed.

As I walked through a field of wheat,
I picked up something good to eat.
It was neither flesh, meat, nor bone,
I kept it till it walked alone.
What is it?
  An egg that hatched into a chicken.

Knock, knock.
Who's there?
Avocado.
Avocado who?
Avocado cold.

Knock, knock.
Who's there?
Cantaloupe.
Cantaloupe who?
Cantaloupe tonight, my father knows about us.

Knock, knock.
Who's there?
Honeydew.
Honeydew who?
Honeydew you think you could open the door
and let me in?

Knock, knock.
Who's there?
Salad.
Salad who?
Salad of bad knock-knock jokes going around!

What turns without moving?
  Milk.

What do you call an egg that just got new eyeglasses?
  Egg-sighted.

What do berry musicians do when they get together?
  They have a jam session.

What do you call an unhappy strawberry?
  A blue berry.

Why did the peanut call the police?
  It was a-salted.

Customer: Is this milk fresh?
Waiter: Yes. In fact, three hours ago it was
     grass.

What smells the best at dinner time?
  Your nose.

72

Did you hear the joke about the guy who had celery sticks in his ears?
Never mind, he didn't hear it either.

What did the one apple say to the other?
"How'd we get out on such a limb?"

Why did the baker quit making doughnuts?
He was tired of the "hole" business.

Why did the boy put the hero sandwich in his eye?
Because his mother said that his eyes were bigger than his stomach.

Why didn't the frankfurter enter the hot dog contest?
He was already a "wiener."

How do police officers like their vegetables?
Grilled.

Mother: You are what you eat.
Little girl: If that's true, I'm not eating my vegetables!

Why is it impossible to starve in the desert?
Because of all the sand-which-is there.

What do you call an angry cabbage?
   A stewing cabbage.

Why couldn't the baseball team drink their soda pop?
   They lost the opener.

What do you call an egg that does death-defying acts?
   A dare-deviled egg.

Did you hear the old jokes about the corn chips?
   Never mind, they're stale.

What side of an apple gets the reddest?
   The outside.

What do you call a stolen spud?
   A hot potato.

What do you call a melancholy lemon?
  A mellow yellow.

Knock, knock.
Who's there?
Kumquat.
Kumquat who?
Kumquat may, we'll always be friends.

What do you call a baby grapefruit?
  A little squirt.

Why do good peach parents put their children in preserves?
  So they don't get spoiled.

What does a nut say when it sneezes?
  "Cashew!"

Why are restaurants dangerous?
  You might bump into a man eating tuna.

What do you call a jogging cashew?
  A health nut.

How did the cashew describe the peanut?
  "That's him in a nutshell."

If potatoes have eyes and corn has ears, what do tomatoes have?
  Each other.

Did you hear about the 500-pound omelette?
    It was an eggs-aggeration.

Knock, knock.
Who's there?
Omelette.
Omelette who?
Omelette you get away with it this time!

How do we know that ants play football?
    Because they're always in the sugar bowl.

Why are bakers rich?
    Because they have all the "dough" they "knead."

Why was the apple so unpopular?
    He was rotten to the core.

What is the invisible man's favorite drink?
    Evaporated milk.

What animals didn't enter the ark in pairs?
   Worms. They entered in apples, not pears.

If peaches grow bigger in fruit trees, where do trousers grow bigger?
   In the pant-ry.

Did you hear the joke about the coconut in the tree?
   Never mind, it's way over your head.

Potato: Good morning!
Farmer: I didn't know potatoes could talk!
Tomato: Neither did I.

Have you ever seen vegetables play ball?
   No, but I've seen a salad bowl.

How do you test an egg?
   Give it an eggs-am.

What do you call a very good egg?
  Egg-cellent.

Why do skeletons drink a lot of milk?
  It's good for their bones.

Customer: Do you serve crabs?
Waiter: Yes, sir, we serve anyone.

Why was the salad dressing in such a hurry?
  It was "rushin.'" (Russian)

What's worse than finding a worm when you're eating an apple?
  Finding half a worm.

Boy: Down on our farm we have a hen that laid
      an egg 6 inches long! Can you beat that?
Girl: Yes, with an eggbeater.

If two apples are a couple of apples, what are two pears?
　　A pair.

What did the gelatin say to the custard?
　　"You're puddin' me on."

What kind of crackers make you smart?
　　Wise crackers.

What can't you eat for dinner?
  Breakfast.

Why was the custodian at the pretzel factory fired?
  He tried to straighten things up.

Patient: Doctor, I get a pain in my eye every
    time I drink my coffee.
Doctor: Next time, try taking the spoon out of
    the cup first.

What bird is always with you at lunch?
  A swallow.

What can you call a potato for short?
  Spud.

What do you call a low-calorie potato?
  Spud light.

Why does a New Year's resolution resemble an egg?
Because it's so easily broken.

Why does an oyster resemble a man of good sense?
Because it knows when to keep its mouth shut.

What would you get if you stacked hundreds of pizzas on top of each other?
A leaning tower of pizza.

What kind of book is the most stirring?
A cookbook.

Why was the bread fired?
He was loafin'.

What's another name for bread?
Raw toast.

Did you hear about the 100-year-old egg?
  Never mind, it's an old yolk.

What's a frog's favorite soft drink?
  Croak-a-cola.

Why did the apple turn over?
  She saw the jelly roll.

What do you eat at breakfast but drink at dinner?
  Toast.

Customer: Waiter, do you charge for bread and water?
Waiter: No, sir, of course not.
Customer: Then that's what I'll have.

What do you call a hot dog at the North Pole?
  A chilly dog.

What do eggs do to keep in shape?
  Eggs-ercise.

First man: Why do you have a pickle behind
    your ear?
Second man: Oh, I must have eaten my pencil
    at lunch.

When is it socially acceptable to drink milk from a saucer?
    When you're a cat.

Why can't Cinderella play volleyball?
    Because she has a pumpkin for a coach.

Knock, knock.
Who's there?
Apple.
Apple who?
Knock, knock.
Who's there?
Orange.
Orange who?
Orange you glad I didn't say apple?

Boy: Do you know why Sam calls his girlfriend
        'candy bar'?
Girl: Because she's sweet?
Boy: No, because she's half nuts.

What do skeletons say before each meal?
    "Bone-appetit."

What does a Martian put in his cocoa?
  Mars-mallows.

What did the man do when his wife made him a marble cake?
  He took it for granite.

Customer: Waiter, there's a hair in my drink!
Waiter: That's impossible. We just shaved the ice this morning.

What do you call someone who eats all the shrimp?
  Shell-fish.

Can you name five things that contain milk?
  Butter, ice cream, cheese, and two cows.

What did the raisin say to the cinnamon roll?
  "I'm rolling in dough."

Why was the cooking class empty?
   The teacher said, "Take one egg and beat it."

What's the best way to sneak up on a gorilla?
   Put on something yellow and pretend you're
   a banana.

Why don't snakes need silverware?
   Because they already have forked tongues.

What do you call a cat that eats lemons?
A sour puss.

What does a nervous cow give?
Milk shakes.

What do moon astronauts drink?
Crater-ade.

What is Oliver Twist famous for?
Pretzels.

How do witches like their eggs?
Terri-fried.

How do you pare a bunch of apples?
Divide them up into groups of two.

What letter of the alphabet can spell potatoes all by itself?
O. Just keep putting O's in a row until you have put-eight-O's.

Knock, knock.
Who's there?
Cashew.
Cashew who?
Cashew see it's me?

What is a witch's favorite dessert?
   Devil's food cake.

Bill: Can you eat with your feet?
Phil: Well, most people can't eat without them!

What's invisible and smells like bananas?
   A monkey burp.

What is a vampire's favorite ice cream?
   Vein-illa.

Why is a waitress sometimes like an umpire?
When someone orders pancakes she yells,
"Batter up!"

What should you do if you don't like the price
of sugar?
Raise cane!

Girl: I know a place where we can eat dirt cheap!

Guy: But I don't like dirt.

What do you call the person who drives the ice cream truck?
A sundae driver.

What do you call twin porcupines?
A prickly pear. (pair)

Why did the piecrust go to the dentist?
It needed a filling.

Girl: Do you know the difference between your hat and that apple?

Boy: No, what?

Girl: Good, then you eat your hat and give me that apple.

How do you make a jelly roll?
Push the jam off the table.

Have you seen a can of pop cook?
No, but I've seen a baking soda.

What has teeth but never eats?
A comb.

How many bananas can you eat on an empty stomach?
One. After that your stomach isn't empty.

First baseball fan: Can you eat a foot-long by
　　yourself?
Second baseball fan: That depends on its shoe
　　size.

What do you get when you cross a chicken with a poodle?
Pooched eggs.

How are dog biscuits made?
With collie-flour.

Knock, knock.
Who's there?
Wiener.
Wiener who?
Wiener you going to let me in?

Teacher: If I have two sandwiches and you have
    two sandwiches, what do we have?
Student: Lunch!

Why did the elephant resign?
    He was tired of working for peanuts.

What is hot, yet always has ice in it?
    Spice.

What is a shoemaker's favorite dessert?
    Peach Cobbler.

How do you carry water in a strainer?
    Freeze it.

Why did the girl take the prune to the dance?
  Because she didn't have a date.

What's the best way to make a buck fast?
  Don't feed it.

Knock, knock.
Who's there?
Justin.
Justin who?
Justin time for dinner, I hope.

Knock, knock.
Who's there?
Hester.
Hester who?
Hester any food left?

Why did the cannibal leave the table?
He was fed up with people.

What makes the leaning tower of Pisa lean?
It never eats.

How do we know that people eat more than dinosaurs?
There are more people than dinosaurs.

What did one pony say to the other pony?
   "You eat like a horse."

Where was breakfast invented?
   Eggsandbay, Conn.

What's the healthiest city in the United States?
   Vita, Minn.

Where can you find the worst leftovers?
   Garbage, Kans.

Where can you almost always find kidney beans?
   Chile.

Where should you take your oranges if you want marmalade?
   Jamaica. (jam maker)

What's yellow and flickers?
  A lemon with a loose connection.

What's Noah's favorite fruit?
  Pears. (pairs)

What's the best way to make pop cold?
  Put ice in his bed.

Jenny: You know, the price of candy keeps
    going up, but the bars keep getting smaller.
Lenny: We should go into the candy business.
    We could make a mint!

What wears a cap but has no head?
  A pop bottle.

What do you call someone who is crazy about chocolate?
  A cocoa-nut.

Why are orange slices so uptight?
  They keep getting chewed out.

What do little icicles call their fathers?
  Popsicles.

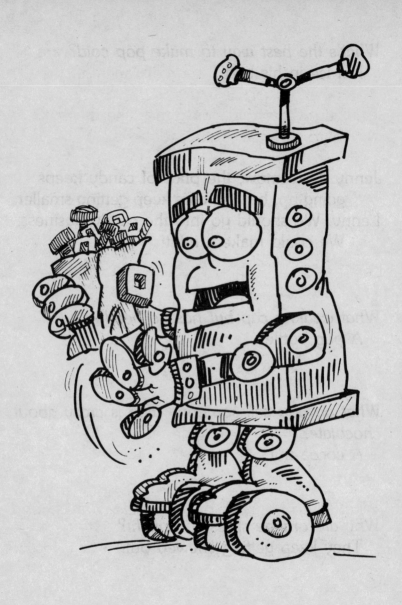

What snack does a robot like best?
Assorted nuts.

Woman: Those sausages you sold me were meat at one end and corn meal at the other!

Butcher: Ma'am, in hard times like these it's hard to make both ends meat!

What food is served every Fourth of July?
Crackers and pops.

How much water can a two-quart colander hold?
None.

What starts with T, ends with T, and is full of T?
A teapot.

What has hundreds of legs, eats, drinks, and flies?
The school cafeteria.

What's red and dangerous?
A herd of stampeding apples.

What's green and makes loans?
  First National City Pickle.

What fruit is found on coins?
  The date.

What is a raisin?
  A worried grape.

What's red and goes beep beep?
  A strawberry in a traffic jam.

What beans won't grow from seeds?
  Jelly beans.

How do you make gold soup?
  Put in 14 carats. (carrots)

How can you raise a salad?
  With a fork.

Why shouldn't you cry over spilled milk?
  Because it will get too salty.

What do trees like to drink?
  Root beer.

What vegetables are always found in a piece of music?
Beets.

Why did the woman have to go to the hospital after a tomato fell on her head?
Because it was in a can.

How can you tell an elephant from a tomato?
Try lifting it. If you can't get it off the floor, it's probably an elephant.

What fish is served on bread?
A jellyfish.

Why did the ants run along the cracker box?
The instructions said, "Tear along the dotted line."

How do bees earn a living?
They cell their honey.

What animal is the smartest?
Ants. They can always find you when you go on a picnic.

What two garden vegetables fight crime?
Beetman and Radish.

What's a comedian's favorite breakfast cereal?
Cream of Wit.

What do you call a funny book about eggs?
A yolk book.

How do you make a pickle laugh?
Tell it an elephant joke.

What happened when the boy drank eight Cokes?
He burped 7-up.

Who's never hungry on Thanksgiving?
The turkey. He's always stuffed.

Why did the sandwich get a medal?
It was a hero.

Marlene: I saw an egg on a plate in New York City.

Charlene: Where did it come from?

Marlene: A hen.

When can you see an elephant in a box of popcorn?
  Never. They come in Cracker Jacks.

What's the difference between an elephant and a grapefruit?
  An elephant is gray.

How are an egg and a horse alike?
  They both must be broken before using.

How can you recognize rabbit stew?
  It has some hares in it.

What do you call a monkey that eats potato chips?
  A chip monk.

What's the best way to keep lettuce?
  Don't return it.

Which side of a hamburger is the left side?
  The part that isn't eaten.

How do you make a hamburger for an elephant?
  First you get a big bun . . .

What do elephants eat besides hamburgers?
  Canned elephant food.

Which hand do the English use to stir their tea?
  Neither. They use a spoon.

If cheese comes on top of a hamburger, what comes after cheese?
  A mouse.

A cook made two dozen hamburgers. All but eleven were eaten. How many were left?
  Eleven.

How can you catch a wild rabbit?
Make a noise like a carrot.

What passes many hamburger stands without moving?
The highway.

What's orange and half a mile high?
The Empire State Carrot.

Who invented spaghetti?
Somebody who really knew how to use his "noodle."

When does a monkey chase a banana?
When the banana splits.

Country girl: Every morning I have eggs for breakfast. I don't have any chickens, and I don't get the eggs from anyone else's chickens.
City girl: Where do you get the eggs?
Country girl: From my ducks!

What smells most at a hamburger stand?
　Your nose.

Why did the elephant sit on the marshmallow?
　To keep from falling into the hot chocolate.

What do you call the boss at the dairy?
　The big cheese.

Why do elephants wear bright green nail polish?
   So they can hide in the pea patch.

What time is it when you divide a pie equally among four children?
   A quarter to one.

How can you track an elephant in the jungle?
   By the smell of peanuts on its breath.

What did the salad say to the spoon and fork?
   "You get me all mixed up."

Why was the butter bad?
   Because when it was cream it wasn't whipped enough.

Why is thunder like an onion?
   It comes peal on peal.

Why did the butcher put bells on his scale?
   Because he wanted to jingle all the weigh.

What is a prize-fighter's favorite drink?
  Punch.

What's purple and 5,000 miles long?
  The Grape Wall of China.

What do you get when you cross a cow with a duck?
  Milk and quackers.

How do you make an elephant float?
  Two scoops of ice cream, some root beer, and an elephant.

What looks like half a hamburger?
  The other half.

Why did the girl sit in front of the television set with milk and sugar?
  She heard there was going to be a serial. (cereal)

What does a worm do in a cornfield?
  She goes in one ear and out the other.

Why is the highest apple on a tree always the best one?
  Because it's the tip top apple.

Why is an ice cream cone like a race horse?
  The more you lick it, the faster it goes.

How can you tell if elephants have been in your refrigerator?
  By the footprints in the butter.

What's yellow, black, and hot?
  Shark-infested mustard.

What comes on a stick and weighs three tons?
  A hippopopsicle.

How can you improve the taste of salt?
  Sprinkle it over hamburger.

What do ghosts eat for lunch?
  Boo-loney sandwiches.

Why was the cornstalk angry at the farmer?
  Because the farmer kept pulling its ears.

What kind of bars can't keep prisoners in jail?
  Chocolate bars.

Why did the boy put dirt in his shoes?
  He wanted his corns to grow.

Mary: What do monsters eat?

Harry: Things.

Mary: What do monsters drink?

Harry: Coke, because Things go better with Coke.

If you lose your knee, where can you get another?

At the butcher shop where kid-neys (kid knees) are sold.

Why do cowboys keep their saddles on the stove?

So they can ride the range.

What kind of cracker is an ice pick?

A water cracker.

What's an anteater's favorite pizza topping?

Ant-chovies.

What happens when you cross an elephant with a jar of peanut butter?

You get a peanut butter sandwich that never forgets.

What kind of apes grow on vines?
  Gray apes. (grapes)

What has antlers and eats cheese?
  Mickey Moose.

What do you get if you cross a potato with an onion?
  A potato with watery eyes.

If you take off my skin I won't cry, but you will. What am I?
  An onion.

If you raise corn in dry weather, what do you raise in wet weather?
  An umbrella.

What does an elk take for indigestion?
  Elka-Seltzer.

What did the baker do when she ran out of strawberries?
  She made strawberry shortcake.

Who's the thirstiest person in the world?
The one who drank Canada Dry.

If you saw a brown egg in a green box on a red table, where did it come from?
From a chicken.

What do you get if you cross a banana with a comedian?
Peels of laughter.

Did you hear the joke about the chocolate cake?
Never mind, it's too rich.

What did Barbie, the play director, do when Chicken Little forgot his lines?
Barbie cued Chicken.

Why did the turkey join the band?
Because it had the drumsticks.

What gives milk, goes "Moo," and makes all your wishes come true?
 Your Dairy Godmother.

Why did the silly farmer bring a needle into the cornfield?
 He wanted to sow the corn.

What fish do they serve on airplanes?
 Flying fish.

What's good on a roll but bad on a road?
 Jam.

Who wears a crown, lives in a delicatessen, and summons his fiddlers three?
 Old King Cole Slaw.

Where do the people of India go for sandwiches?
 To the New Delhi.

Why do bakers make good baseball pitchers?
Because they know their batter.

What is the highest-ranking vegetable?
Corn kernels. (colonels)

What's the quickest way to make soup taste terrible?

Change the U to an A and you get *soap*.

What musical do pickles like best?

"Hello, Dilly."

Why do potatoes make loyal friends?

They're always there when the chips are down.

What do sweet potatoes do when they play together?

They have a yam session.

What happens when you cross a potato with a sponge?

You get a vegetable that soaks up a lot of gravy.

Why did the banana split?

Because it saw the bread box, the milk shake, and the ginger snap.

How do you make meat loaf?
  Send it on vacation.

What do termites eat for breakfast?
  Oak meal.

What's green, three stories tall, and tastes good on bread?
  The Jelly Green Giant.

What do you call a thief who steals ham?
  A hamburglar.

Where would you use raspberry ketchup?
  On jelly beans.

Why do pessimists hang around delicatessens?
  They expect the wurst.

What's the best way to keep milk from turning sour?
  Keep it inside the cow.

What do you get when you cross a pretzel with a doughnut?
   A whole new twist.

How do pizzas travel?
   They pie-cycle.

Where does the Gingerbread Man sleep?
   Under a cookie sheet.

How many apples grow on a tree?
   All of them.

What do you call 500 Indians without any apples?
   The Indian-apple-less 500.

What do you get when 125 raspberries are trying to get through your door?
   A raspberry jam.

What did the candy bar say to the lollipop?
   "Hello, sucker!"

Why did the cook put the cake in the freezer?
  She wanted icing on it.

What's green and red all over?
  A pickle holding its breath.

What's the oldest fruit?
  Adam's apple.

What's purple and a member of your family?
  Your grape grandmother.

What do squirrels give each other on Valentine's Day?
  Forget-me-nuts.

Where does a pickle factory get its cucumbers from?
  The farmer in the dill.

What vegetable do you find in crowded streetcars and buses?
  Squash.

*What do you get when you cross the
Frankenstein monster with a hot dog?*
   A Frankfurterstein.

What should you do if you meet King Kong?
   Give him a BIG banana.

What cracker invented the telephone?
   Alexander Graham Cracker.

Why were the sardines out of work?
  They got canned.

What Jack tastes good with syrup?
  Flapjack.

Why did the candy factory hire the farmer's daughter?
  They wanted her to milk chocolates.

What's green, thin, and jumps every few seconds?
  Asparagus with hiccups.

How do you straighten crooked apple trees?
  Take them to the orchardontist.

What has 22 legs and goes crunch, crunch?
  A football team eating potato chips.

What does a hungry mathematician eat?
  A square meal.

What swings through the trees and has purple juice all over his body?
  Tarzan of the Grapes.

What do witches eat for breakfast?
  Scrambled hex.

What do you call a drippy vegetable?
  A leek.

What's dark, wrinkled, and makes pit stops?
  A racing prune.

Little girl: Father, may I have another apple?
Father: What! Another apple? Do you think they
    grow on trees?

If cakes are 66 cents each, how much are upside-down cakes?
  99 cents.

What did Mary have for dinner?
  Mary had a little lamb.

Customer: Waiter, there's a fly in this ice cream!
Waiter: Serves him right. Let him freeze!

What kind of soda can't you drink?
Baking soda.

What do you call a hot dog who gives his honest opinion?
Frank.

What do you get if you cross a chef and a rooster?
Cook-a-doodle-do.

What size are very large eggs?
Eggs-tra large.

What fruit do electricians like best?
Currants.

What did the sherbet ask the ice cream?
"Get the scoop?"

127

What's the difference between a zoo and a delicatessen?
   A zoo has a man-eating tiger, and a delicatessen has a man eating salami.

What did one herring say to the other herring?
   "Am I my brother's kipper?"

What did the peel say to the banana?
   "Don't move, I've got you covered!"

What do bees like to chew?
   Bumble gum.

What do you get if you cross an octopus and a cow?
   An animal that can milk itself.

Where do blue Easter eggs come from?
   Sad chickens.

How do you know if your teapot is happy?
   It whistles while it works.